books by Mary M. Isaacs

Christ Child's Lullaby

Holy Innocence

Hidden in Plain Sight

The White Bird

Hair of the Dog

Lux Umbra Dei

The Least of These

Holiday Stories

HOLIDAY STORIES

Thanksgiving to New Year's Eve

Mary M. Isaacs
2023

3

"God bless Us, Every One!"

--Christmas, 2023--

Rosemary for Remembrance

Rosemary for Remembrance

She looked at her table, which she had just finished setting. The burgundy tablecloth was one of her best; there were matching burgundy candles in the crystal candlesticks. She had spent over an hour polishing the silver and washing the best china, after getting it down from the cupboard over the refrigerator. Now she straightened the silver at each place setting and made sure the water glasses had no spots. She wanted everything to look perfect tonight. The dining room had been cleaned and dusted earlier, the windows washed, and the chairs polished. It looked as lovely as she remembered from all Thanksgiving dinners past.

Suddenly the doorbell rang. She turned away from the table expectantly, whisking off her apron as she hurried to the door. She looked through the peephole and then opened the door with a welcoming smile.

A man in uniform stood there, holding a small arrangement of flowers. "Holiday delivery for Andrews?" he asked.

"Yes, that's me," she said, looking at the flowers closely. Red and pink carnations were mixed with small tea roses, with fir, rosemary, and dried statice scattered throughout.

"Kind of an unusual combination, isn't it?" the delivery man said. "But it looks pretty, and it sure does smell nice."

"Thank you," she smiled warmly as she took the arrangement from him. "Wait a minute..." and she picked up a twenty-dollar bill from the small table by the door and handed it to him.

He looked surprised. "Twenty bucks?" he asked, looking at her.

"It IS Thanksgiving Day," she said. "I really appreciate your being able to deliver the flowers fresh today."

"Well, thank you! And Happy Thanksgiving to you and yours!" he said, smiling broadly, and then he turned to walk back to his van.

She closed the door while admiring the flowers. They were just right. Carrying them carefully to the dining room, she placed the arrangement in the exact center of the table. It went beautifully with the tablecloth and the candles in their holders. She knew she had chosen well, even though she had ordered them sight unseen.

All at once she remembered the food cooking. While putting her apron on again, she hurried out of the dining room and into the kitchen. Her track record for cooking turkeys was uneven at best, so for this special occasion she played it safe by ordering a fully cooked one. She had picked it up earlier at the grocery store, during its shortened hours, along with ready-made gravy from the deli.

She checked the potatoes on the stove and the sweet potatoes in the oven. The pie had been made the night before and was sitting on the sideboard, ready to be cut and served. The pouches of frozen petite peas were boiling away on the stove--everything was nearly ready.

11

All she needed to do was pull it all together at the last minute...

* * * * *

At last everything was ready. She carried in the turkey, on its platter, and set it on the sideboard in the dining room. The bowls of mashed potatoes, sweet potatoes, and peas she set on the table, each with its own silver serving spoon. Cranberry jelly glowed in a cut glass dish. The gravy was in a small pitcher, ready to be poured out. Everything was in its place.

She hung up her apron behind the kitchen door, smoothed down the skirt of her best dress, and sat down at the table. After glancing at the empty armchair at the head of the table, she bowed her head and spoke her father's favorite prayer aloud. In the silence that followed, she could almost hear her mother's voice echoing the final "amen".

As she sat alone at the table, she felt the memories of many Thanksgiving dinners wash over her. The smells were right, the food looked perfect, and the table decorations were as beautiful as ever her mother had arranged. The only difference was the flowers--and she

12

had chosen those specifically for this day. *Rosemary for remembrance...* she thought. Other years would be different, but for this first Thanksgiving meal without her parents, she wanted to honor and remember her loved ones in her heart, by herself.

As she lifted her glass in thankfulness for their lives, and toasted her parents silently, she felt again the warmth of their love and affection for her; the close family circle that remained unbroken in her memory, even though they were no longer there.

That was something she would remember every day, not just at Thanksgiving.

Nick at Night

Nick at Night

The coffee shop owner looked up as the door opened. When he saw who had come in, he grinned widely. "Hey, Nick, how's it going?" and then he glanced at the clock on the wall. "You just barely made it on time! I was about to lock up."

The young man walked to the counter. "Sorry, Mr. Collins, but I was kept late at work. I'm glad you're still open. How many were turned in today?"

The owner opened the cash register. From underneath the till he pulled out several laminated red cards. "Eight, Nick," as he handed them over. "All coffee drinkers this time. Pretty nice guys, too—they all said to tell you 'thanks.' Oh, and I wiped those down for you."

"Eight?" replied the young man. "There should be a couple more. I wonder where they are? I hope those guys are okay…" He looked worried.

"Maybe they're saving them for some time special. Maybe they didn't see them and left them behind. Maybe they got lost." The coffee shop owner spoke cheerfully, trying to inject a positive note. "They'll turn up, Nick."

"Maybe so." The young man took the cards and then rummaged in his pocket. "I hope I have enough to cover these, Mr. Collins. Payday isn't until tomorrow." And he started counting out bills onto the counter. The coffee shop owner watched the process anxiously.

The young man finished counting and looked up apologetically. "Gosh, Mr. Collins, I'm so sorry. There's not enough to pay for them all. I should try to plan things out better. I guess I'm not very good at budgeting."

"Don't worry about it, Nick. I know you're good for it." The owner gathered up the money and put it away in the till. Then he shut the cash register drawer. "Are you going out again tonight?"

"Yes. It's going to be extra cold overnight, the weatherman says. They'll need something to warm them up in the morning."

"Well, then, you'll need something too. I'll make you a hot chocolate. You can pay me tomorrow." The coffee shop owner started fixing a hot drink for the young man.

"Thank you, Mr. Collins. And don't forget to let me know if you need some extra cleaning done before I come in Saturday morning."

The coffee shop owner nodded and then handed over the hot chocolate. The young man took it to one of the small tables, sat down, and opened his shoulder pack. Out of it he pulled several envelopes. He put one of the red cards in each of the envelopes, sealed it, and wrote a few words on the front. Then he put the small stack of envelopes in his jacket pocket. After he finished, he took a little time to enjoy his hot chocolate, looking around the little coffee shop he knew so well. Where should he go tonight, he wondered. He'd already been downtown a couple of times recently. Maybe one of the freeway overpasses? Yeah, that would be good. Maybe a couple of the overpasses. There were some out-of-the-way places there, sheltered places for someone sleeping outside all night.

He gradually realized that the owner was putting things away for the night. The young man got up and helped him to wash the tables and stack the chairs. Afterwards, as he slung on his shoulder pack and was getting ready to leave, the coffee shop owner called him over to the display counter.

"Pick out a couple of doughnuts for the road, Nick— on the house."

"But I already owe you for the chocolate and some of the extra coupons, Mr. Collins."

"You need energy for this job, Nick! Here—this is your favorite kind, isn't it?" He put two oversized jelly doughnuts into a bag. "Take a couple of napkins, too, for spilled jelly."

"Yeah, I know--it always gets all over my chin," the young man laughed. "Thanks, Mr. Collins."

"Happy distributing, Nick—stay safe!"

The owner walked to the door with the young man, clapped him on the shoulder, and then locked the door after him. He watched the young man through the glass door as he walked away into the fading light. *That Nick! He sure is something!* Then he turned around to finish closing up.

....

Early the next morning, the coffee shop owner was busy setting things up for the day. He opened the big boxes of doughnuts that had just been delivered and looked with satisfaction at the tempting contents. He put a couple of jelly doughnuts aside and then filled the pastry trays in the display cabinet.

Just as he finished setting out the doughnuts, a man came into the shop. He was dressed in a business suit and had the air of being a little out of his element. In spite of that, he walked up to the counter expectantly.

"May I help you?" asked the shop owner.

"Well, I hope so," the businessman said. He reached into his inner jacket pocket and pulled out a red card.

The owner's eyebrows shot up and he looked startled. "Are you turning this in?"

"Turning it in?" The businessman looked puzzled for a moment. "Oh! no. No, I'm not here for..." and he read aloud what was printed on the card. " 'A free hot drink of your choice and two doughnuts at Collins' Café' ." He looked up at the shop owner as he handed over the card. "I found this on the street where I usually park my car. Someone dropped it, I imagine. Looked interesting, well-designed, so I thought I'd come and ask about it. Is this some kind of promotion?"

"No, it's not a promotion."

"Well, why do you give these out?"

"I don't give these out."

"But it's from your shop! You have to know how people get these! Is this some kind of scam?"

"No, it's not a scam!" the coffee shop owner answered heatedly. Then he looked at the businessman for a while, trying to decide how much to explain. Finally, something about the man's demeanor helped him make up his mind. "Okay, there's this young guy, see? I've known him since he was a kid. Used to come here with his mama—he liked the jelly doughnuts." The owner laughed. "He'd pick out the goopiest one, and always got the jelly all over his face." He stopped, lost in memories.

"He's not a kid any more, is he?" prompted the businessman.

The shop owner shook himself back to the present. "No, he's grown up now—well, not too grown up! He still lives here, he has a job, and he still likes jelly doughnuts. Anyway, he came in one day with this idea… He saw guys sleeping outdoors all night and it made him feel bad. He knew he couldn't do much to help but figured out a way to do something nice for them. He made up one of these cards—the coupon you brought in?—and asked me if I'd honor them. He'd pay me for every coupon that was turned in, and he said he'd come in once a week and do extra cleaning. He figured that the guys might not be the cleanest in the world—not their fault!—and as the whole thing was his idea, he didn't want me to have to do more cleaning. So that's what it is. He distributes the coupons, the guys bring them in, and they get doughnuts and a hot drink."

"Quite a set-up," said the businessman.

"Yeah, Ni—," the coffee shop owner caught himself. "He's pretty smart. Well, thanks for bringing in the coupon. He'll be glad to know it was just lost. He knows exactly how many he gives out, and it bothers him when some are missing. He worries about the guys he gives them to. Hey, how about a cup of coffee on the house? As an appreciation for bringing in the coupon."

"A cup of black coffee would be fine, thank you. I have a few minutes before I have to be at work."

"Go ahead and sit down anywhere. I'll bring it to you."

The businessman walked over to a small table by a window. He sat down and looked around the shop. It was small but home-y. He liked being there and wondered why that was. There was nothing special about the furnishings or the décor, but there was just— something. It was just a nice place.

The owner came to the table with a large cup of coffee. "Black, like you wanted. But if you change your mind, there's cream and sugar on that shelf there." After setting down the cup, the owner turned to go back to work—but his eye was caught by movement outside the glass door. Someone was standing there, looking at something he held in his hand; something red.

The coffee shop owner strode to the door and opened it. "Hey, is that one of our coupons? Come on inside!" He held the door open and ushered the man in, almost by sheer strength of will. "Would you like some coffee? Tea? Hot chocolate? Here, put your stuff down at this table and come pick out your doughnuts. There's a lot to choose from this morning—not too many customers yet!"

The man went over to a table and set down a backpack and bedroll. Then he met the coffee shop owner at the counter and handed him the red card. "I found this on the ground beside me when I woke up this morning."

"Just passing through?" The owner asked.

"No, I live here. Well, here and there…"

"I understand, man. I see your bedroll. Coffee?" The homeless man nodded in reply. "Which doughnuts would you like?" The owner filled a large coffee cup as he spoke.

The man looked at the doughnuts. "These all look really good. I can have any two I want?"

"Sure," the owner said, "anything you like."

After a few moments' deliberation, the homeless man indicated two bars—maple- and chocolate-covered.

"Good choices!" said the owner, as he put them on a plate and handed it over the display cabinet. "And here's your coffee. Cream and sugar are over there," he indicated the shelf.

The homeless man took his doughnuts to the table, set the plate down, and walked over for cream and sugar. He then sat down and began on one of the doughnuts.

The shop owner continued to set up for the day. He brought plates and cups out of a small kitchenette behind the counter and stacked them, ready for use. He refilled utensil containers and wiped down the serving area. From time to time he glanced at the two men in the shop; after a while he took the coffee pot to offer refills. The businessman accepted more coffee, and then the owner went to the other occupied table. He saw with satisfaction that one of the doughnuts was gone. "Good doughnuts, right?" he said, and held up the pot.

The homeless man nodded and pushed his cup over for the refill.

As the owner poured more coffee, the homeless man asked, "Who does this? The coupons, I mean. Is it you?" The coffee shop owner shook his head. "Then who does it?"

"Sorry, man, I can't tell you that. But he's a good guy."

"Yeah," the homeless man took a drink of his coffee. "A really good guy."

The shop owner returned to the counter and busied himself between there and the kitchenette. The businessman sipped at his coffee and alternated between watching the homeless man and watching the owner. The homeless man ate the second doughnut and drank his coffee. It was quiet and peaceful in the shop.

When he had finished, the homeless man brought his cup and plate to the counter and then returned to the table and started to gather up his things.

"Wait," the shop owner called over to him. "You get a takeout sandwich, too." And he started pulling supplies out of a refrigerator.

"I do?" the homeless man was surprised. The businessman shifted in his seat and took another drink of his coffee, watching over the rim of the cup.

"Sure—what kind would you like? Turkey? Ham? Roast beef?"

"Wow—roast beef would be great, thank you."

"Whole wheat or white bread? And all the fixings?"

"White bread, please. And lettuce and tomato, if that's okay."

"Cheddar cheese?"

The homeless man nodded and then looked around him. The coffee shop owner pointed to the far corner of the shop. "Bathroom's over there. This'll be ready for you in a jiffy."

As the man went towards the bathroom, the shop owner continued to prepare a big sandwich. He also wrapped up a large dill pickle and got a small bottle of water from the refrigerator. He put all the items into a paper bag. The businessman watched silently.

After finishing, the owner walked to the end of the counter and leaned over some equipment. All of a sudden, soft Christmas music began to play. At the same time, the homeless man returned from the bathroom and put on his backpack. He stopped and listened for a moment, and then said, "That's right—Christmas is coming soon."

The coffee shop owner walked over with the bag. "Here's your sandwich. I hope you enjoy it."

"I will, thank you!" The homeless man smiled and took the bag. "And please thank that guy who gave me the coupon." He then picked up his bedroll and left the shop.

The owner walked to the door to watch him go. Then he got a wet rag and cleaned off the table where the man had been sitting, and straightened the chairs. When he finished that, he returned to the counter and started clearing away the sandwich makings. When he finally turned around, the businessman was at the counter looking at him.

"Would you like anything else? Coffee refill? A doughnut maybe?" the owner asked.

"A sandwich isn't on the coupon," the businessman said, matter-of-factly.

The coffee shop owner shrugged. "It's just part of the deal."

"I don't think so. That's all you, isn't it? Your contribution. Does the other guy know about that?"

"No, he doesn't--and he's not going to know! I'm just paying it forward. The other guy, he's the one. It was all his idea, right from the start. HE goes out at night and gives out the coupons. HE knows where the homeless folks are. HE comes in here and does extra cleaning, just in case the coupon guys track in dirt or whatever. He does all the work. But I've seen how it makes people happy, so--I just wanted to help."

"Me, too," said the businessman, and he pulled a wallet from his back pocket. He took out a bill and handed it to the café owner. "Here—sandwiches for the next few coupons that are redeemed. My treat." Then he turned and walked out the door.

The shop owner watched him go, in surprise, and then finally looked at what he held in his hand. It was a hundred-dollar bill.

He stared at it for a few moments, and then grinned widely. *That Nick! His idea just keeps getting bigger and better!* He put the bill and the red card into the cash register and went to clean the table by the window. The Christmas music continued playing as the owner hummed along:

"In the bleak mid-winter/Frosty wind made moan;
Earth stood hard as iron/Water like a stone;
Snow had fallen, snow on snow/Snow on snow,
In the bleak mid-winter/Long ago....

What can I give Him/Poor as I am?
If I were a Shepherd/I would bring a lamb;
If I were a Wise Man/I would do my part,
Yet what I can I give Him/Give my heart."

From the carol, "In the Bleak Mid-Winter"; lyrics by Christina Rossetti, music by Gustav Holst.

The Christmas Card

The Christmas Card

It's like herding cats! Linda thought with a smile.
Fortunately, she loved cats—almost as much as she
loved the little children standing together in front of
her. She was trying to line them up on the low platform
that had been set up for them, and get them into order
by height. They were wiggling and giggling, as always—
both eager to begin and a little shy of the strangers who
were coming into the room.

Her Sunday School primary class (3- to 5-year-olds)
had come to this nursing home to sing a few Christmas
songs. For several weeks they had practiced and had
also been busy making Christmas cards to hand out.
The cards were made from all colors of construction
paper, folded over, with stickers and drawings and their
names, too, in various stages of legibility. Linda would

have liked to add glitter—both she and the children loved it—but the nursing home had requested its absence. Linda recalled the first year she had come with her class for this singing, bringing along well-glittered cards. She clearly remembered how the glitter had mysteriously multiplied and spread itself all over the nursing home. She had volunteered to help clean it up. It had taken hours...

This year's unglittered cards were stacked in a basket on the floor near her. After the children had sung their Christmas carols, they would hand out their cards to the residents of the nursing home, who were now taking their places in the large room. The children's parents were already sitting in folding chairs along the wall at the back, but the residents were still walking in, using canes, walkers, or moving slowly on their own two feet. One side of the room had many armchairs. Some were already occupied; it looked like they all would be, soon. The other side of the room had been kept clear. Orderlies were pushing in other residents who were in wheelchairs, filling up the empty space in rows.

Linda had been bringing her Sunday School children to this nursing home for several years, at Christmas and Easter. The classes looked forward to it. It was an exciting trip to an unfamiliar place, and they loved singing together. And of course, they fully enjoyed making their cards.

Finally, one of the administrators told her that everyone was there who was able to be there. Linda thanked her and then spoke to the children. She told them that it was just about time to begin. Several of them got scared looks, especially the youngest ones, but Linda smiled at them. "You all look so nice, and they will love to hear how beautifully you're going to sing!" She meant it, too—she was so proud of them. They had all dressed in their best for this visit. The boys were in shirts with ties, some even with suit jackets. The girls had fancy Christmas dresses, and some had sparkly bows in their hair. Linda felt a rush of love in her heart as she looked at them.

She turned and introduced them to the residents. "We hope you will enjoy our songs!" she added. "If you know the words, please sing along with us!" She then turned back to the children, whispered "Jingle Bells", and raised her hand for a 1-2-3 countdown. The program had begun!

Of course, most of the residents sang "Jingle Bells" along with the children, and of course the children sang it as they always did, with a lot of enthusiasm. Linda had picked that song to be first for those very reasons. She had the children sing it through several times, to give all the older people a chance to join in if they wanted to. The children were thrilled to hear their audience singing with them. Linda had anticipated that, too.

When they finally stopped singing "Jingle Bells", many of the residents clapped and made comments about how nice it was (some of them kept singing a little longer, but Linda knew that would happen. *Let them enjoy themselves—they're having a good time!*) The children's parents clapped, too.

The children were delighted by the reception they got and sang the rest of their songs with spirit: "Away in a Manger", "We Wish You a Merry Christmas", "Rudolph the Red-Nosed Reindeer", and "Silent Night". The residents loved every moment, and joined in singing every song. Linda felt that they would appreciate an encore, so she had the children sing "Jingle Bells" one more time. This time everyone sang, including all the parents. Their combined voices filled the room with warm feelings.

After all the voices had quieted down, Linda picked up her basket and addressed the residents. "The children have been very busy making Christmas cards for you. And they are going to give them to you, right now, and wish you a Merry Christmas!" She picked up the card on the top of the pile and read the signature. "Allie?" she called out and looked at the group of children. One of the pretty Christmas dresses stepped out of the lineup on the platform and took the card. Allie walked over to an elderly woman in a wheelchair and handed her the card. "Merry Christmas!" she said and smiled shyly. The older woman took the card but looked right into the girl's eyes. "Thank you, dear—and Merry Christmas to you, too!" Then Allie skipped to the back of the room and stood by her mother.

Linda picked up the next card. "James?" The tallest boy in the back row grabbed the card and gave it to a man sitting in one of the chairs, with a greeting and a grin. The older man took the card and said, "Merry Christmas! Such a fine young man!" James looked proud as he walked back to his parents.

One at a time, Linda gave cards to the children and the children delivered them to the residents. She always started with the older ones now. Many of them had done this before, either at Easter or Christmas last year, so they knew what to do. The younger children could watch them and later follow their lead. Years ago, Linda had tried to start with the younger children, but most of them had become completely shy or scared. *You live and learn!* she reminded herself.

Soon, most of the cards had been handed out. Linda called one little girl's name and handed her the card she'd made. But the three-year-old stayed put, shaking her head. Linda bent over her and asked quietly, "Do you want to take your card home, Katie?" Sometimes a child wanted to do that; Linda never forced them to give it away. But the little girl shook her head even harder. "It's for the grandpa," she whispered, looking anxious.

"You want to give it to your grandpa?" Linda asked her in a lowered voice.

The little girl frowned and said, "No—the grandpa here!"

Linda said, "Oh, the grandpa *here*! Is he in this room?" Another shake of the head was the only answer. "Is he somewhere else in this place?" The little girl nodded and looked pleadingly at Linda. "Should we go find him when this is over?" More nods and the beginnings of a smile. "Okay, why don't you go sit with your daddy now, and we'll look for the grandpa later." The little girl smiled hugely as she clutched her card and ran to sit on her father's lap.

The rest of the cards were given out, but Linda still had a few in her basket. "A couple of our Sunday School children couldn't be here today, but they made extra cards—is there anyone who didn't get one yet?" A few people raised their hands and Linda gave each of them a card, with a personal "Merry Christmas from Robby!" or "from Grace" or "from Andrew", whichever name was written on the card.

When everyone had received a card, Linda said, "Thank you all for coming to our program! Merry Christmas to each one of you, and God bless you!" The residents slowly got up to leave or were pushed out in their wheelchairs. Many of them exchanged Christmas greetings with the children and their parents as they passed by them. Linda picked up her belongings and followed slowly, glad to see the interactions. After all the residents were gone, the parents helped their children put on their coats. Linda thanked them for coming. "I'll see you next Sunday, in church school!"

she added, as they left the room with their excited, happy children.

Linda waited until the room was nearly empty, and then she turned to the small girl and her father. "Katie says she saw a grandpa here who wasn't in this room, and she wants to give her card to him." She looked at Katie's dad questioningly. "Do you know who she means?"

He looked puzzled for a moment and then said, "Maybe... When we came in the front door, there *was* a man lying on a movable bed in the entry hall. Katie seemed fascinated by seeing a bed that wasn't in a bedroom, and she asked a lot of questions." He looked down at his daughter. "Is that who you want to give your card to, honey? The man in the bed on wheels?"

"Yes!" said Katie, as she slipped off her father's lap and took his hand.

"Well, let's go find him!" said Linda. She put on her coat, put her purse in the basket, and they left the room.

The three of them walked down a long corridor. As they came to the entry hall, Katie's face suddenly glowed. A wheeled bed was parked against the wall; a man was lying on it. His eyes were closed and his arms were tucked under the blanket. His chest rose and fell regularly, Linda noted, thanking God....

"Is this the grandpa you were talking about, Katie?" Linda stooped down and asked quietly. Katie looked up at her with a big smile and a nod, and then looked back at the man on the bed.

Linda said, "I think he's asleep right now, but I know he'll love looking at your pretty card when he wakes up."

Katie's dad picked her up and brought her close to the bed. She leaned over her father's arm and put her card on the man's blanket, right over his heart. Her face was very happy. "Merry Christmas! I love you," she said in a whispery voice. Then she snuggled against her father and leaned her head on his shoulder, still smiling at the man on the bed.

Linda looked over at Katie's dad in surprise. He smiled at her, and then kissed his little daughter. "Come on, honey, it's time for us to go home."

Katie took her eyes off the man and looked at her teacher. "Bye, Miss Linda!" she said with a little wave.

"Good-bye, Katie—I'll see you next week!" Linda replied. She watched as the man and the child walked across the entry hall and out the door.

After a moment, she turned back to look at the sleeping man. He was still breathing quietly; Linda carefully repositioned the card so that it wouldn't fall off his chest. *I wonder what he'll think when he wakes up and finds the card,* she thought. *Will he know that a tiny little angel has been here?*

She smiled gently to herself--and then she, too, walked to the door and left.

Christ Child's Lullaby

Christ Child's Lullaby

Rose hurried, so she wouldn't miss the beginning of the church service. It was already too late for her to take her place in the choir—she couldn't have, anyway, because of the cold and laryngitis that had crept up on her the past several days. She knew it was coming and it made her heart sink. There was nothing Rose loved more than singing, and she especially looked forward to Christmas time when she could sing the beautiful music she had adored and sung since childhood. She knew she had a good voice—her friends told her that, choir directors told her that, even strangers in church said so. That didn't matter, one way or another. She just loved to sing; she would sing even if her voice had been plain and ordinary.

She buttoned up her overcoat and put on a woolen cap, gloves, and snow boots. It was bitterly cold outside, and the forecast had called for more snow sometime before morning. Even though it was too late to protect her voice from the cold, Rose still needed to keep warm. The church was very large; good for singing but bad for warmth. As she was not going to be in the relatively sheltered group of singers standing shoulder-to-shoulder, but instead sitting in a cold wooden pew by herself, she needed the heavy outer clothing.

She remembered to turn the heat down in her small apartment. She also left a few lights on, as her parents had advised when she moved to the city. After locking the door, she hastened down the stairs and out through the glass doors of the lobby. No one was around—too cold, too late at night. Everyone was either snug at home, or already where they were going for the evening. She turned at the corner and made her way down several blocks, avoiding icy patches and leftover drifts of snow. It had been a rough week for weather, so she was careful how and where she stepped.

The bulk of the old church soon loomed on her left. She saw a few people climbing the stairs and pulling open the heavy wooden doors. She followed them, entering the quiet darkness of the narthex; there were candles burning there and also inside the sanctuary. An older man greeted her and handed her a bulletin. She looked at it as she made her way to a side aisle and seated herself at the end of a pew. The church was partly full. The service began almost as soon as she sat down…

Rose loved every moment—even the times when the choir sang alone, when she should have been singing with them. The words of their special music echoed in her heart and she imagined herself singing along. It was almost enough, but still she felt a little sad. When the congregation stood for the Christmas carols, she stood, too. After the first words of the first carol, when her voice came out as a broken whisper, she didn't try to sing any more, but let the words and music flow around and through her. She *thought* the words, remembering all the years before of singing these beloved songs. *Next year, next year; it will be better next year*, she promised herself--*next year I will sing and sing, every song!* But she had a few tears. Her throat hurt and she controlled her coughing as much as possible.

In between songs and Scripture readings she looked around. The familiar church looked especially lovely in

49

candlelight. It was so large that the ceiling was shrouded in darkness. The wood of the old, worn pews glowed in the dim light. There was a large painting on a side wall close to the front, of Mary holding the child Jesus on her lap. The light from so many candles made the image flicker a little, giving the impression of faint movement, as of breath. Mary's eyes seemed to look right at her, sending comfort and strength, as though she knew all about Rose's impaired voice. A wave of love came to her as she looked at the painting.

Many people sat around her. Some looked familiar, from Sunday services (although she only knew the choir members, somewhat). However, as it was the last Sunday before Christmas Eve, there were people she had never seen before—some shabby, some looking troubled or sad, others looking serene and happy. Each face held different emotions. Young and old, rich and poor, all were represented in the gathering. All had come, like Rose, to experience the hushed time of waiting and expectation.

The service came to an end and most of the people began to depart. The lights remained off as the celebrants and congregation left in candlelight. Rose noticed a few people remaining seated, in prayer or quietly waiting in the shadows.

Preparing to leave, her eyes were caught again by the painting of Mary and her son. Deep within her, she heard a silent request, a request for her to stay. Although unspoken, it was strong and compelling; Rose remained standing, facing forward, as she listened to the sweet voice inside her. After a few moments, something moved her to leave the pew and walk up the aisle toward the front of the church. Towards the painting. As she came closer, the image grew clearer and richer.

She glanced at the pews around her as she walked past. By this time they were empty, except for a few people scattered here and there. They all seemed absorbed in thought or prayer. She knew most of them slightly—there was the young woman who had shared, over coffee hour, that her husband had left her. She sat hunched over, holding her face in her hands. Farther away was the man who had been giving out the bulletins. Rose remembered that he had been laid off from his job only a week or two ago. *What an awful time of year to be unemployed*, she thought. She walked past an older woman who was crying silently, tears spilling down her face. Her hands were grasped together tightly.

51

Across the aisle was an elderly couple, sitting close to each other. Rose knew they were in fragile health and were very worried about that. *How did they manage to get here safely, through the icy streets?* she asked herself. A young man sat quietly, with his eyes closed. Rose recognized him from past Sundays, but she was always too shy to speak to someone she didn't know, even though he looked nice.

She finally reached the front of the church. She stopped a few feet from the painting and waited quietly, looking straight into Mary's eyes. The voice came again…

"Sing to my Son for me."
"But my voice is gone," Rose whispered sadly.
"Sing to my Son for me."
"My lady, I can't!" tears gathered in Rose's eyes and began to fall.
"Yes, you can. Please sing to Him."

Rose looked down and was silent for a moment; she then raised her head, took a deep breath, and began to sing. Her heart soared, higher and higher, as she sang. It was like being lifted to the stars.

"My son, my treasured one are you,
My sweet and loving son are you,
You are my love, my darling, new--
Unworthy, I, of you.
Alleluia, alleluia, alleluia, alleluia."

While Rose sang the old Scottish lullaby, a small part of her wondered at how she no longer had laryngitis, at how strong and clear her voice was. But mostly she was focused entirely on the song, the words, the emotions. Her grandmother had sung this lullaby to her countless times when Rose was a little girl. While she sang it, she remembered being held close in her grandmother's arms as she slowly drifted off to sleep. It was the right song, the perfect song to sing to baby Jesus, the Christ child.

Mary's eyes in the painting shone in the candlelight as the song words floated, high and clear, throughout the church. A sense of peace blanketed everyone there. The elderly couple looked at each other lovingly and moved closer together, clasping each other's hands. Their worries and fears subsided as they rested in the beautiful music. The young woman whose husband had left her raised her head in surprise; a look of hope and strength slowly grew on her face.

"Your mild and gentle eyes proclaim
The loving heart with which you came--
A tender, helpless, tiny babe
With boundless gifts of grace.
Alleluia, alleluia, alleluia, alleluia."

While the song continued, the older woman sitting alone felt a strong impulse to look at her phone. She pulled it out and then stared in near-disbelief at the number on the display. With tears blurring her vision, she quickly put on her coat and hurried toward the main door of the church. As she left, her face shone with a look of love almost matching the one on Mary's face. The man who had passed out the bulletins stopped gathering them up, closed his eyes, and offered a prayer of thanksgiving. He knew, deep in his heart, that God was watching over him and would provide him with all he needed, every day.

"King of kings, most Holy one,
God the Son, eternal one,
You are my God—and helpless son--
High Ruler of mankind.
Alleluia, alleluia, alleluia, alleluia."

The young man leaned over his folded hands, with a joyful smile on his face. He recognized that voice—he had heard it every Sunday, part of the choir but still distinct and set apart. That voice had touched his heart, but he couldn't tell who the singer was. Now he knew. It was the young woman he had noticed at coffee hour. He had wanted to introduce himself to her but hadn't quite found the right time or way. Now he looked up at the figure of the girl standing in front of the portrait of Mary and Jesus. It was like finding a long-lost friend. It had been difficult and discouraging for him, moving to an unfamiliar city without friends or family. He now felt very glad to be living here.

The lullaby ended. The last note shimmered in the air, and Rose looked into Mary's eyes. It seemed to her that the painted smile deepened for an instant—and then the feeling of being uplifted slowly faded away and departed. Rose turned and started walking back to the pew where her coat was.

As she walked, she saw the remaining people quietly preparing to leave the church. After putting on her coat, she went to help the elderly man, who was having a little trouble bundling his wife up in her overcoat. They thanked her for her help and then all three walked to the door, Rose matching her pace to their slower steps. By the time they reached there, the church was empty. In the narthex, however, she saw the young man, who was obviously waiting for them.

"Do you have a car? It's snowing outside," he said to the older couple. When they answered in the negative, he asked, "May I call a taxi for you?" The couple thanked him, and the young man made the call. They waited inside until the taxi arrived, and then he and Rose helped the older couple down the church steps, which were now covered with snow. They assisted the man and his wife into the taxi, closed the door, and watched while the car pulled away from the curb and drove off.

The young man looked at Rose. "How are you getting home? Do you need a taxi, too?"

She answered, "Oh, no, I live only a couple of blocks from here. It's just a short walk."

"But it's a cold and slippery walk," he responded. "May I see you home? I wouldn't want you to fall and hurt yourself."

Rose looked at him for a moment, and then smiled. He was a stranger—but also not a stranger. She had seen him in church, often, and he had helped the old couple. She wasn't quite sure why, but she trusted him. "Thank you. I live down that way," she said, pointing. "Oh--my name is Rose."

"I'm Joe," the young man said, and he held out his elbow for her. She put her arm through it and they walked off together, slowly and carefully, avoiding icy patches and the fresh drifts of snow.

Note: "The Christ Child's Lullaby" is an English translation of a much longer traditional Gaelic Christmas song, "Taladh Chriosda," from the Outer Hebrides of Scotland.

Dark and Cold is the Night

Dark and Cold is the Night

Dark and cold is the night--
High above, a star shines bright.
Far down below in the stable small,
A young woman cradles the hope of all.
She rocks her child to sleep
While angels vigil keep.

He is Lord of the earth,
Yet he had a humble birth.
No silken sheets to caress his form,
Only some hay to keep him warm.
She holds her baby tight--
She guards him in the night.

Angels appear in the skies,
Glory bursts on shepherds' eyes!
Hastening back to Bethlehem town,
Finding the manger and kneeling down.
The love of God for all
Rests in a child so small.

Gifts from over the sands,
Carried in the Wise Men's hands:
Gold is the gift for a mighty King,
Frankincense for worshiping,
And myrrh...to mark his death.
His mother holds her breath.

Dark and cold is the night--
High above, a star shines bright.
Far down below in the stable small,
A young woman cradles the hope of all.
She rocks her child to sleep
While angels vigil keep.

Stephen's Feast

Stephen's Feast

Owen was on his way home, tired and hungry after a long day at work. It was the day after Christmas, but someone had to staff the office even though it was usually a very quiet day. He had volunteered, so that all his married colleagues could spend an extra day home with their families. There was no one for him to celebrate with, not even a dog, so he didn't mind coming into work right after the holiday.

The weather wasn't looking good; it had been cloudy all day, with a couple of brief showers, but now it was threatening heavy rain. It would be a long drive home, as he lived over 25 miles away from the office--freeway driving most of the way, but always slow and tricky in bad weather. *Better stop and get some dinner now, he thought. Maybe that BBQ place—yeah, that would taste good! I'm really hungry. I'll get a BBQ sandwich meal for tonight and an extra sandwich for tomorrow's lunch. And maybe an extra side—two are never enough. Their sides are good enough for a meal on their own… I just hope they haven't run out of anything!*

He reached the BBQ place and turned into the parking lot. He went inside, breathing in the delicious smell as soon as he opened the door. As he stood in line, he went through the usual uncertainty of which of the sides he would order. They offered six, but he knew he should limit himself to three. By the time he reached the front of the line, he had decided on the mac and cheese and the cole slaw, with corn muffins extra. As he was ordering, though, he kept thinking about the fries. *Regular or sweet potato? I'm so hungry…* The young boy behind the counter waited patiently while Owen thought, clearly used to patrons' indecision about sides. "And regular fries, too," Owen finally announced. As he waited for his order to be assembled, he noticed that some light rain was starting to fall. Owen added a large cup of coffee to his order, realizing that it could be a while before he reached home, and he might need it.

Owen paid for the food and the full bag was handed over. He left the BBQ place and hurried to his car, dodging raindrops. He considered putting the bag on the seat next to him, so he could snack on the fries at least, but decided to wait until he got home. If he put it behind his seat, he wouldn't be tempted to eat while driving. *Man gets into accident on the freeway while eating cole slaw during rainstorm; details at 11*, he laughed to himself.

It wasn't far from the BBQ place to the freeway. As he approached the on-ramp, he saw a hitchhiker by the entrance, holding a cardboard sign that read, "Porterville". He knew that city was about 150 miles to the north. *Bad night for hitchhiking such a long distance*, he thought. And the man had no umbrella or overcoat, just a yellow rain poncho over his shoulders. Owen passed him by, heading north on the freeway—but continued to think about the man, sitting on the side of the road as a rainstorm was just about to hit. Abruptly, he got off at the next exit, turned left onto the overpass, and got back on the freeway heading south. At the next exit, he repeated the moves. Owen pulled to the side of the road right at the on-ramp and honked at the hitchhiker, who quickly got into the car, carrying a small shoulder pack. Owen told him he was going about 25 miles north, towards Porterville, and would drop him at the freeway entrance where he turned off.

He got back on the freeway just as it started to rain harder. The hitchhiker peered out through the windshield and said, "Looks like this'll be coming down for a while. Thanks for picking me up."

The man was shivering slightly. "Pretty cold out there, right?" Owen asked. He turned the heat up in the car. Glancing sideways, Owen saw that the hitchhiker was on the thin side and looked very tired. "Take off your poncho if you like," he told the man. "Saw your sign-- Porterville. How long you been on the road?"

The hitchhiker pulled the poncho off, rolled it up, and shoved it down by his feet. "I left Madison City early this morning. I was hoping to make it to Porterville by nightfall, but haven't had many rides, and most of them were short. I guess the weather hasn't helped." He looked out the window again as the rain increased.

After a moment, Owen remarked, "I haven't been to Porterville for a long time."

"I've never been there. But my sister lives there, with her family. We've talked on the phone. She's happy there; sounds like a nice place. I wanted to surprise her and make it there by Christmas. Didn't manage that, but I called her and let her know that I was on my way.

She said that'd be a pretty nice Christmas present." He paused for a moment. "I haven't seen her in a long time. Years," he added. He looked over at Owen and said, "Thanks for picking me up. Maybe I'll make it there tonight after all."

"No problem. By the way, my name's Owen." He took one hand off the wheel and held it out to the other man while introducing himself.

The man grinned. "Very glad to meet you, Owen. I'm Steve." They shook hands and then settled back into a comfortable silence.

The rain came down harder and Owen put the windshield wipers on high; they made a hypnotic sound as they swept from side to side. He wondered to himself what was going to happen to his passenger if he didn't make his destination that night—because it seemed more than likely that he wouldn't. Owen turned on the CD player; soft instrumental Christmas music filled the car. "That's nice," said Steve, and then he took a deep breath. "Sure smells good in here," he said.

"I stopped for some BBQ sandwiches," Owen said. "You want one? Reach behind my seat and get the bag."

"I can't eat your dinner," Steve replied. "What will you eat then?"

"Don't worry, I bought two sandwiches. There's one to share."

"Well, if you're sure...thanks." Steve reached behind Owen's seat and carefully lifted the heavy bag and put it on his lap. He opened it and got out one of the wrapped sandwiches.

"There should be a fork and napkins in there, and some sides. They always come with sides. Help yourself to anything—I'm not very hungry, but they always include sides, so I take them."

Nodding his thanks, Steve started in on the sandwich. He ate rather quickly. He must be really hungry, Owen said to himself. Then he remembered something. "Here, better have this coffee too. It'll be cold before I can get it home." He lifted the covered cup out of the cup holder and handed it to the man.

"Thanks a lot," Steve said as he grasped the cup, uncovered it, and took a drink before putting it back into the holder. "Hey, man, God bless you. I haven't had much to eat today. This is really nice of you." He finished the sandwich and started to open the container of one of the sides. It was the mac and cheese; Owen tried not to look as Steve finished it off and started on the cole slaw, while drinking the coffee. He went by that BBQ place twice a day during the week—he could always get more. He was glad he had something to share.

The light had almost faded completely by now and the rain was coming down in sheets, off and on. Owen kept his eyes on the road and the rear-view mirror for the next few miles. There wasn't much traffic, but visibility was bad and there was always the chance of a skid with the roads this wet. While he concentrated on driving at a safe, reduced speed, he wondered how his passenger would manage to get a ride in this pouring rain. *No one will want to pick him up this time of night--he'll be dripping wet and it'll be dark. He'll have to sleep under the overpass, or at a bus stop or something. He might even get sick.* He considered this for a while, and then turned to Steve to ask him what his emergency plans were. But Steve

71

had fallen asleep, still holding the empty coffee cup. Owen reached over, gently took it from his hand, and put it in the cup holder. Steve didn't stir. *Long day, full stomach, warm car—he'll sleep for quite a while, I think. He probably really needs that.*

Owen continued to drive in silence, with only the sound of the windshield wipers to accompany his thoughts. Just then, he saw a mileage sign—½ mile to his turnoff, 125 miles to Porterville. *Only a couple hours more. IF he gets a ride.* Owen looked over at the sleeping man again, frowning slightly.

Without being fully conscious of his decision, he drove past his exit and continued north on the freeway. *With any luck, he'll sleep most of the way, so no arguments— and he'll be rested, ready to see the family. They'll still be up, maybe, and be glad to see him.* Owen smiled, thinking about Steve seeing his sister again, after years of separation. *It won't be too long of a ride back. Anyway, I like driving.*

He continued down the road, navigating carefully through the downpour. But even through the rain, he could see many strings of colored lights on either side of the road--still brightly shining, this first day after Christmas.

72

Auld Lang Syne

Auld Lang Syne

"All beautiful the march of days/As seasons come and go.

The hand that shaped the rose has wrought/The crystal of the snow,

Has sent the hoary frost of heav'n/The flowing waters sealed,

And laid a silent loveliness/On hill and wood and field..."

Rose peered through the small window in the heavy wooden door of the old church. No taxi yet, just gently falling flakes of snow in the late afternoon light; she was glad the snow had held off until after the service was over. It would be a light snowfall, though, like the recent ones, and she could have walked to the church service; it was only a few long blocks, after all, and there was no ice. But Mrs. Evans had insisted that she take a taxi there and back, and Rose had agreed in order to give her neighbor peace of mind. Not like last year, after that memorable Advent service—and she smiled to herself as the memory flooded back. Joe had walked her home that evening, through the fallen snow. But Joe wasn't here today to hold out his elbow for her arm to guide her steps home. She missed him, and wished he was there.

It was New Year's Eve. The special late afternoon church service—sparsely attended because it was mid-week, with a big night to come—had ended a little while ago. Although the congregation was small, those who attended sang whole-heartedly, Rose among them, in honor of the coming new year. The priest announced that there would be a special ringing of the church bells at midnight, to mark the passage of the old year and the arrival of the new.

Rose had stayed to help straighten up the prayer books and hymnals and collect any leftover bulletins for the trash. The man who usually did that was unable to get off early from work, so she had volunteered to take his place. While she was busy, the other attendees had left, calling out New Year's greetings to each other. Now she was alone—well, not quite. Members of the altar guild were setting up for the coming Sunday morning service. She would have liked to offer to help them, or even just observe with questions, as she hoped to join that group in the new year. But Mrs. Evans was waiting for her at home; they were going to have New Year's Eve dinner together. Mrs. Evans was cooking the meal and Rose knew that food preparations had started hours ago. So she had called a taxi and was now waiting for its arrival.

While she waited she thought of Joe. Ever since that Advent service, a year ago, he had been part of her life-- a special part. Slowly at first: properly, carefully. He had spoken to her at the church's coffee hours, listened to her choir rehearsals, sat with her when the choir wasn't taking part in the service. He walked her home in bad weather. When she volunteered for church clean-up days, he volunteered also. And then he invited her for lunch at a café—and a visit to a museum—and a warm spring day at the zoo. Over the months, they spent more and more time together. He told her about his job, his family, his dreams. She listened with interest and encouragement. He praised her singing and told her that that was the first thing he ever knew about her: her beautiful voice in the church choir. She had blushed when he spoke well of her voice, but he had been so kind, so sincere. They had spent time together increasingly through the year—and now she missed him at this special church service. But Joe had gone to his family's home for Christmas. He had planned to be back by New Year's, but an unexpectedly heavy storm in the area where his family lived had changed those travel plans.

A car pulled up to the curb, interrupting her memories. Rose could see that it was from the taxi company she had called. She pulled her knit cap down more snugly and slung her handbag over her shoulder. Opening the heavy door, she stepped outside and took hold of the stair railing firmly. She slowly descended the stairs and carefully crossed the sidewalk. The steps weren't slippery at all, but Rose didn't want to chance a fall in the fading light. She climbed into the taxi, gave the driver her address, and then took out her wallet. It wasn't going to cost much, as she was going only a short distance, but it was nice not to have to walk. She'd have to thank Mrs. Evans for insisting that she ride!

When the taxi arrived at her apartment building, Rose handed the driver her fare, with a tip folded inside. As she pulled on the door handle, the driver got out, surprisingly, and came around and helped her out of the taxi. "It's getting a little dark. Gotta see you safe to your door—bad night to call for an ambulance, New Year's Eve and all!" he said cheerfully. He escorted her up her building's steps and then said, "Good-bye— Happy New Year!" She returned the greeting and then watched as he got back into his taxi and drove away. When she could see the car no more, she opened the glass door and went inside.

She pulled off her coat and cap in the entryway. Carrying them, she went up the short flight of steps to the first floor where her apartment was located. Before she reached her door, however, she could smell something good coming from across the hall, from where Mrs. Evans lived. Rose smiled as she anticipated another traditional, old-fashioned holiday meal like her grandmother used to make. As soon as she unlocked her door and went inside, she turned up the heat and switched on some lights; her apartment was cold and dark. She was thankful that she would not have to spend New Year's Eve alone; she would be having dinner with a friend.

"O'er white expanses, sparkling pure/ The radiant morns unfold;

The solemn splendors of the night/ Burn brighter through the cold.

Life mounts in ev'ry throbbing vein/ Love deepens round the hearth,

And clearer sounds the angel hymn/ 'Good will to all on earth.' "

Right after Christmas, Rose had realized that the caregiver who usually helped her older neighbor hadn't been around for a while. She wondered why that was, as Mrs. Evans definitely needed regular help. Rose had gone across the hall to her neighbor's apartment and asked about the caregiver directly.

"Oh, Julia can't come for a while. Her husband slipped that day we had some ice on the ground, and sprained his ankle. She has to stay home for a while and take care of him," her neighbor had replied in response to Rose's question.

"Who has been helping you with cleaning and laundry?" Rose had asked.

"Well, no one, really. I clean up as best I can…"

80

Both women had looked around the small apartment then. Rose noticed the dust and the unswept floors and then thought quickly. "Maybe I can help you, Mrs. Evans, until Julia is able to come back or you find someone else. And what about food? How have you been managing without her doing your grocery shopping?"

Fortunately, Mrs. Evans told her, the caregiver had just done the weekly shopping before her husband's accident, so the refrigerator and pantry cupboards were reasonably well-stocked. "And I am still able to cook, although I'm not good for much else!" she added, laughing.

"I have an idea, Mrs. Evans," Rose had said. "Why don't we eat together until Julia's husband is better and she can come back? You can cook our meals, and in return I'll clean your apartment, go grocery shopping for us both, and do your laundry along with mine. How does that sound?"

"What a dear girl you are, Rose. You won't mind spending your time with an old lady like me? What about your young man?"

Rose had blushed a little. "Joe flew home to spend Christmas with his family. He would have been back by now, but some big storms shut down the airport there. So---you don't have someone to help you and I'm home all day for a while, too. My school is closed for the holidays, so I don't have to go to work for at least another week. Let's share our responsibilities and keep each other company until Julia gets back." They both agreed to this plan, and their friendship had grown deeper through the unexpected adversity.

....

Rose hung up her coat and cap in the entryway closet and then went into the kitchen. Earlier that day she had made an apple pie and had left it to cool while she went to the church service. Along with some ice cream that she had on hand, it would be a splendid dessert treat for their New Year's Eve dinner. She hadn't told Mrs. Evans of her baking plans—it was going to be a surprise. She'd offered to bring a salad, which she now proceeded to assemble. There was still some fresh fruit from her last shopping trip; she'd use it all and make a colorful, beautiful salad. After New Year's Day she could go to the local grocery store, for herself and for her neighbor. There was plenty of food for tonight and tomorrow. Rose was grateful for whatever was put on the table—she wasn't picky. She was just thankful for God's provisions to her, through Mrs. Evans and their friendship.

While she was finishing the salad, she heard her apartment bell ring. She wiped her hands on a dishtowel and went to the door. She called out, "Who is it?" as her parents had requested that she do, instead of opening her door to just anyone who might be there. Slightly muffled sounds came through the door, and she recognized her neighbor's voice.

She had barely started opening the door when Mrs. Evans began to speak. "Oh, Rose, I'm glad you're home safe from church. I worried about you the whole time you were gone!" A short, elderly woman stood there, smiling up at the girl. "You took a taxi back, too, right?" and she stepped inside as Rose opened the door wider for her.

"Yes, Mrs. Evans, I did--and the driver was very nice. Because it was getting dark, he helped me up the stairs to the door of our building."

"Oh, my, that was thoughtful of him," said the older lady. Then she closed her eyes briefly and sniffed the air. "What smells so good?" And she looked up at Rose with a twinkle in her eye.

"Surprise!" said Rose, "I made an apple pie to top off our dinner tonight. And I have some vanilla ice cream, too."

"Oh, thank you, Rose! That will be a special treat for celebrating the New Year! I expect your pie will be delicious. I'm sorry your young man can't be here to enjoy it with us."

Just at that moment, the phone in Rose's kitchen rang. She looked puzzled. "I guess that's my parents calling on the landline. They insisted I have one, in case of trouble with any of our cell phones, but I talked to them before I went to church. Strange…" And she went to pick up the phone. As she got closer, she saw the last name on the display. "Oh!" she said, in a surprised and delighted tone of voice. "I think it's Joe!"

Mrs. Evans turned and walked back to the apartment door. "You'll want some privacy," she said. "Let me know when you finish your call. Dinner is almost ready to put on the table. Don't forget to bring that pie and ice cream!" She went out into the hall and closed the door behind her.

Rose smiled gratefully as she picked up the receiver. "Hello?" she said eagerly. The phone crackled in her ear and she moved it away an inch or two until the noise stopped. Then she spoke again. "Joe? Is that really you? I'm glad you called."

His voice came through, broken up a little by static. "Rose? I'm calling from my parents' phone. Can you hear me? I can barely hear you."

She smiled at the familiar tones of his voice. "Yes, Joe, I can hear most of what you are saying. But why are you calling from their number? What happened to your cell phone?"

"The cell towers are down here, because of the storm, and your cell phone wasn't picking up," he replied. "Good thing I had your other phone number! Otherwise I couldn't have gotten through at all."

"I'm glad you did, too. I thought it was my parents calling—but it's you…" and she smiled again. "Are you having a good time with your family? I went to the New Year's Eve church service this afternoon—I missed you being there, Joe." She added shyly.

There was a sudden burst of static, making it hard for her to hear him. Then all at once his voice came through clearly. "…how is the weather there, Rose? Are you okay?"

"Yes, Joe, I'm fine. The weather isn't bad here at all, not like where you are."

She heard crackling on the line, and then his voice again. "…wanted to be there…talk to you tonight, but…storm…"

"I'm sorry you're not here, too, Joe, but I'd rather know that you're safe. Anyway, you'll be back soon, after the storms stop. We'll see each other then."

More static interrupted the connection. She strained to hear his voice, which cut in and out. "…wanted to ask…this year…not much time left."

Rose smiled. "No, just a few hours. But why is this year so important? Next year is just tomorrow. It's not a long wait."

"…don't want…wait…ask…this year." There was a silence on the line; Rose thought she heard him take a deep breath, but it could have just been the bad connection. "Rose…I love…marry me?"

The phone popped and crackled and she strained to hear his words. She held the phone tighter than before, as if she could get closer to him to hear what he was saying. "What did you say, Joe? The connection is so bad…"

"Will you marry…?" and then his voice was cut off.

"Yes! Yes, yes, yes, yes, yes!" she said, desperately hoping that one of her words would make it through the static. But there was silence from the other end. "Joe? Can you hear me? I love you too, Joe! Yes, I will marry you! Are you there, Joe?" The silence continued, interrupted by crackles and hisses—and then the line went completely dead.

Rose held the phone to her ear a while longer until she remembered that he'd never get through again unless she hung up. She put down the receiver and gripped both hands together, watching the display. She waited a long time, but nothing happened. *Oh, Joe!* she thought. *Did you hear me at all? Did you hear me say 'yes'?* She looked up at the clock on the wall. It was still this year! There were a few hours left before midnight. Maybe he would be able to get through again soon. Tears filled her eyes and started to fall—tears from a mixture of joy and frustration.

87

At that moment, her apartment bell rang again. Rose walked unsteadily to the door and opened it, tears still rolling down her cheeks. Mrs. Evans started speaking again before the door was open. "I just wanted to see if you'd finished your call…" and then she saw the girl's face. "Rose! Oh, my dear, what's the matter? Tell me…oh, no--did something happen to Joe?"

"No, no, Mrs. Evans, Joe is all right. It's just…that…that…he said…he asked me to marry him, Mrs. Evans! But the line went dead! I don't know if he heard me say 'yes'." And Rose broke down crying. "I don't even know if he heard me say I loved him!"

The older woman put her arms around Rose and held her in a warm embrace. "Of course he heard you, dear. Everything is going to be all right, you'll see. Oh, I am so happy for you! Joe is a fine young man—so nice and polite and caring. You are just right for each other! Take this," she said briskly, handing Rose a handkerchief from her pocket, "Now let's go ahead and have our dinner. We'll move everything over here, to your apartment! Then you can hear if your phone rings--if he calls, we'll just stop eating while you talk! And if the bad weather there blocks any more calls, then it's no good worrying about it and sitting around doing nothing but waiting. We'll have our lovely New Year's Eve dinner and maybe watch a holiday movie. Then it will be close to midnight, and time to celebrate! And what a lot there is to celebrate, to be sure."

Rose dried her eyes and mopped her face. "Thank you, Mrs. Evans. You make me feel much better. Your plan sounds just fine. Shall I come with you to bring the dinner over?"

"We'll take turns, dear, so one of us can answer the phone here if it rings. Let me go first and bring some of the food—then you can get the place settings and the tablecloth. It shouldn't take too many trips to bring everything over here. Then we'll have our blessing and get started. I want to get everything out of the way so I can have a piece of that lovely pie you made!"

Rose laughed then, just as Mrs. Evans had hoped. "We're not going to hurry through your delicious meal just for a piece of pie! Dessert comes last," and she watched the older woman go across the hall.

In a short time, everything for the dinner had been brought over from Mrs. Evans' apartment and set up on Rose's dining table. Both women sat down and then joined hands; Mrs. Evans asked Rose to lead them in a blessing for the meal. Rose began and her neighbor joined in, both women singing the words to the tune of the Doxology, singing from their hearts: *"Be present at our table, Lord/ Be here and everywhere adored/ These mercies bless and grant that we/ May strengthened for thy service be. Amen."*

They talked steadily through the meal. Mrs. Evans gently led Rose to recalling things about Joe and sharing her thoughts and hopes for the future. The phone didn't ring during dinner but talking about Joe helped Rose to relax and stop worrying, which was what her neighbor intended. They finally reached the end of the meal, and Rose brought in the apple pie and ice cream. Both women had two servings of the dessert, and then sat back in their chairs, completely full and satisfied.

"What a very nice meal we just had!" The older woman smiled lovingly at the younger one. "Thank you so much for sharing your food and yourself with me, dear Rose! I haven't had such a lovely New Year's Eve in a long, long time."

Rose smiled back at her and then said, "I'll help you carry the leftovers home to put in your refrigerator, Mrs. Evans, but leave the dirty dishes here. I'll wash them and bring them over to your apartment tomorrow."

The women took turns carrying food to the other apartment, and then they both rinsed the dishes and stacked them on Rose's kitchen counter. Afterwards, they settled into the living room and watched "Miracle on 34th Street" with much enjoyment. Both had seen the old movie many times before and shared their favorite parts with each other. When the movie was over, it wasn't yet midnight, but Mrs. Evans decided it was time for her to go home.

"I can hardly keep my eyes open! Too much pie, I guess," and she winked at Rose. "You'll have to see the New Year in without me." She stood up, and Rose accompanied her to the door. When they got there, Mrs. Evans gave the young woman a big hug. "Happy New Year, dear. May it be filled with happiness and blessings—like you've given me."

Rose kissed her cheek. "Good night, Mrs. Evans, and Happy New Year to you, too! Sleep well--I'll see you in the morning for breakfast." And she watched the older woman cross the hall and go into her apartment safely. When the door had shut, and Rose heard the bolt being drawn into place, she went back into her apartment and started washing the dishes. She fully intended to stay up until long past midnight, just in case Joe would be able to call, so she decided she had enough time to wash and dry everything and tidy up for the night.

When she finished in the kitchen it was close to midnight. She went to the living room window, opened it partway, and stood there, breathing in the crisp, cold air. Although she was a couple of blocks from the church, she knew she was usually able to hear the bells, and she really wanted to hear them this night, ringing in the New Year. But instead, she heard a different kind of ringing. It was the phone! She ran to it, hoping that it wasn't her parents, although she wouldn't mind wishing them a happy New Year. But it was Joe, calling again! She grabbed up the receiver, her heart pounding.

"Hello?" she said breathlessly. This time there was no static. Joe's voice sounded clear and she could hear every word.

"I didn't imagine it, did I, Rose? You really said 'yes'?"

She burst into tears. "Yes, Joe, I really said that! I love you, Joe. I'm so glad you were able to call again tonight!"

"Dear heart, please don't cry. I wish I was there, but it's almost midnight and this phone call will have to do... Rose, I have a ring here for you. Hold out your left hand." Rose quickly switched hands holding the receiver and did as she had been asked. "Imagine this, Rose: I'm putting the ring on your finger right now. I love you and I want us to be together forever."

"I love you, too, Joe. It's a beautiful ring, and it fits perfectly." She smiled through her tears as she made the gentle joke--which wasn't a joke at all, of course. It had always been a perfect fit between them; she knew that he'd understand what she was saying.

"Rose, I'll be there as soon as I can be. As soon as this storm eases up and the planes are flying again. The weatherman says three days, maybe. But that's a long time..." his voice trailed off briefly. "I'll call you every day, Rose. Don't go outside if the weather gets bad there. Do you have enough food? Has the power stayed on the whole time so far?"

"Yes, Joe, everything is fine here. My neighbor Mrs. Evans and I have been sharing our meals and spending time together. Between the two of us we have enough food to get by for a few more days, and we keep each other company. She's nice, Joe. And she likes you..."

93

"If she's sharing with you, being there with you, I like her, too."

Rose looked at the clock again. Was it midnight yet? No, it was still this year, but just barely; the second hand glided toward the twelve. She smiled and waited silently through the last few seconds. The church's bells would ring loudly and joyfully when the time was up, and she would hear them clearly, just as she was hearing Joe's words clearly this call. She was filled with happiness.

Seven...six...five...four...three...two...one... She took a deep breath as she heard the pealing of the bells through the open window. "It's midnight now, Joe. Happy New Year! God bless you!"

"A happy and blessed New Year to you, my dear love—no, to us!" he responded. "I'll be there with you soon."

Her heart soared and sang along with the bells...

"...O God, from whose unfathomed Law/The year in beauty flows,

Yourself the vision passing by/In crystal and in rose,

94

Day unto day shall utter speech/And night to night proclaim,

In everchanging words of light/The wonders of your name."

Hymn lyrics from "All Beautiful the March of Days" by Frances Whitmarsh Wile, ca. 1907 (usually sung to the tune of "Forest Green").

"God rest you merry, gentlemen, let nothing you
dismay/Remember Christ our Savior was born on
Christmas Day..."

[18th-century English carol]

Made in the USA
Las Vegas, NV
18 September 2023

77763560R00058